ADIEU

LECTOR HOUSE PUBLIC DOMAIN WORKS

This book is a result of an effort made by Lector House towards making a contribution to the preservation and repair of original classic literature. The original text is in the public domain in the United States of America, and possibly other countries depending upon their specific copyright laws.

In an attempt to preserve, improve and recreate the original content, certain conventional norms with regard to typographical mistakes, hyphenations, punctuations and/or other related subject matters, have been corrected upon our consideration. However, few such imperfections might not have been rectified as they were inherited and preserved from the original content to maintain the authenticity and construct, relevant to the work. We believe that this work holds historical, cultural and/or intellectual importance in the literary works community, therefore despite the oddities, we accounted the work for print as a part of our continuing effort towards preservation of literary work and our contribution towards the development of the society as a whole, driven by our beliefs.

We are grateful to our readers for putting their faith in us and accepting our imperfections with regard to preservation of the historical content. We shall strive hard to meet up to the expectations to improve further to provide an enriching reading experience.

Though, we conduct extensive research in ascertaining the status of copyright before redeveloping a version of the content, in rare cases, a classic work might be incorrectly marked as not-in-copyright. In such cases, if you are the copyright holder, then kindly contact us or write to us, and we shall get back to you with an immediate course of action.

HAPPY READING!

ADIEU

HONORE DE BALZAC,
KATHARINE PRESCOTT WORMELEY

ISBN: 978-93-5342-176-2

First Published: -

© LECTOR HOUSE LLP

LECTOR HOUSE LLP
E-MAIL: lectorpublishing@gmail.com

ADIEU

BY

HONORE DE BALZAC

TRANSLATED BY
KATHARINE PRESCOTT WORMELEY

DEDICATION
TO PRINCE FREDERIC SCHWARTZENBURG

CONTENTS

ADIEU

CHAPTER I.

AN OLD MONASTERY

"Come, deputy of the Centre, forward! Quick step! march! if we want to be in time to dine with the others. Jump, marquis! there, that's right! why, you can skip across a stubble-field like a deer!"

These words were said by a huntsman peacefully seated at the edge of the forest of Ile-Adam, who was finishing an Havana cigar while waiting for his companion, who had lost his way in the tangled underbrush of the wood. At his side four panting dogs were watching, as he did, the personage he addressed. To understand how sarcastic were these exhortations, repeated at intervals, we should state that the approaching huntsman was a stout little man whose protuberant stomach was the evidence of a truly ministerial "embonpoint." He was struggling painfully across the furrows of a vast wheat-field recently harvested, the stubble of which considerably impeded him; while to add to his other miseries the sun's rays, striking obliquely on his face, collected an abundance of drops of perspiration. Absorbed in the effort to maintain his equilibrium, he leaned, now forward, now back, in close imitation of the pitching of a carriage when violently jolted. The weather looked threatening. Though several spaces of blue sky still parted the thick black clouds toward the horizon, a flock of fleecy vapors were advancing with great rapidity and drawing a light gray curtain from east to west. As the wind was acting only on the upper region of the air, the atmosphere below it pressed down the hot vapors of the earth. Surrounded by masses of tall trees, the valley through which the hunter struggled felt like a furnace. Parched and silent, the forest seemed thirsty. The birds, even the insects, were voiceless; the tree-tops scarcely waved. Those persons who may still remember the summer of 1819 can imagine the woes of the poor deputy, who was struggling along, drenched in sweat, to regain his mocking friend. The latter, while smoking his cigar, had calculated from the position of the sun that it must be about five in the afternoon.

"Where the devil are we?" said the stout huntsman, mopping his forehead and leaning against the trunk of a tree nearly opposite to his companion, for he felt unequal to the effort of leaping the ditch between them.

"That's for me to ask you," said the other, laughing, as he lay among the tall brown brake which crowned the bank. Then, throwing the end of his cigar into the ditch, he cried out vehemently: "I swear by Saint Hubert that never again will I trust myself in unknown territory with a statesman, though he be, like you, my dear d'Albon, a college mate."

"But, Philippe, have you forgotten your French? Or have you left your wits in Siberia?" replied the stout man, casting a sorrowfully comic look at a sign-post about a hundred feet away.

"True, true," cried Philippe, seizing his gun and springing with a bound into the field and thence to the post. "This way, d'Albon, this way," he called back to his friend, pointing to a broad paved path and reading aloud the sign: "'From Baillet to Ile-Adam.' We shall certainly find the path to Cassan, which must branch from this one between here and Ile-Adam."

"You are right, colonel," said Monsieur d'Albon, replacing upon his head the cap with which he had been fanning himself.

"Forward then, my respectable privy councillor," replied Colonel Philippe, whistling to the dogs, who seemed more willing to obey him than the public functionary to whom they belonged.

"Are you aware, marquis," said the jeering soldier, "that we still have six miles to go? That village over there must be Baillet."

"Good heavens!" cried the marquis, "go to Cassan if you must, but you'll go alone. I prefer to stay here, in spite of the coming storm, and wait for the horse you can send me from the chateau. You've played me a trick, Sucy. We were to have had a nice little hunt not far from Cassan, and beaten the coverts I know. Instead of that, you have kept me running like a hare since four o'clock this morning, and all I've had for breakfast is a cup of milk. Now, if you ever have a petition before the Court, I'll make you lose it, however just your claim."

The poor discouraged huntsman sat down on a stone that supported the sign-post, relieved himself of his gun and his gamebag, and heaved a long sigh.

"France! such are thy deputies!" exclaimed Colonel de Sucy, laughing. "Ah! my poor d'Albon, if you had been like me six years in the wilds of Siberia—"

He said no more, but he raised his eyes to heaven as if that anguish were between himself and God.

"Come, march on!" he added. "If you sit still you are lost."

"How can I, Philippe? It is an old magisterial habit to sit still. On my honor! I'm tired out—If I had only killed a hare!"

The two men presented a rather rare contrast: the public functionary was forty-two years of age and seemed no more than thirty, whereas the soldier was thirty, and seemed forty at the least. Both wore the red rosette of the officers of the Legion of honor. A few spare locks of black hair mixed with white, like the wing of a magpie, escaped from the colonel's cap, while handsome brown curls adorned the brow of the statesman. One was tall, gallant, high-strung, and the lines of his pallid face showed terrible passions or frightful griefs. The other had a face that was brilliant with health, and jovially worth of an epicurean. Both were deeply sun-burned, and their high gaiters of tanned leather showed signs of the bogs and the thickets they had just come through.

"Come," said Monsieur de Sucy, "let us get on. A short hour's march, and we shall reach Cassan in time for a good dinner."

"It is easy to see you have never loved," replied the councillor, with a look that was pitifully comic; "you are as relentless as article 304 of the penal code."

Philippe de Sucy quivered; his broad brow contracted; his face became as sombre as the skies above them. Some memory of awful bitterness distorted for a moment his features, but he said nothing. Like all strong men, he drove down his emotions to the depths of his heart; thinking perhaps, as simple characters are apt to think, that there was something immodest in unveiling griefs when human language cannot render their depths and may only rouse the mockery of those who do not comprehend them. Monsieur d'Albon had one of those delicate natures which divine sorrows, and are instantly sympathetic to the emotion they have involuntarily aroused. He respected his friend's silence, rose, forgot his fatigue, and followed him silently, grieved to have touched a wound that was evidently not healed.

"Some day, my friend," said Philippe, pressing his hand, and thanking him for his mute repentance by a heart-rending look, "I will relate to you my life. To-day I cannot."

They continued their way in silence. When the colonel's pain seemed soothed, the marquis resumed his fatigue; and with the instinct, or rather the will, of a wearied man his eye took in the very depths of the forest; he questioned the tree-tops and examined the branching paths, hoping to discover some dwelling where he could ask hospitality. Arriving at a cross-ways, he thought he noticed a slight smoke rising among the trees; he stopped, looked more attentively, and saw, in the midst of a vast copse, the dark-green branches of several pine-trees.

"A house! a house!" he cried, with the joy the sailor feels in crying "Land!"

Then he sprang quickly into the copse, and the colonel, who had fallen into a deep reverie, followed him mechanically.

"I'd rather get an omelet, some cottage bread, and a chair here," he said, "than go to Cassan for sofas, truffles, and Bordeaux."

These words were an exclamation of enthusiasm, elicited from the councillor on catching sight of a wall, the white towers of which glimmered in the distance through the brown masses of the tree trunks.

"Ha! ha! this looks to me as if it had once been a priory," cried the marquis, as they reached a very old and blackened gate, through which they could see, in the midst of a large park, a building constructed in the style of the monasteries of old. "How those rascals the monks knew how to choose their sites!"

This last exclamation was an expression of surprise and pleasure at the poetical hermitage which met his eyes. The house stood on the slope of the mountain, at the summit of which is the village of Nerville. The great centennial oaks of the forest which encircled the dwelling made the place an absolute solitude. The main building, formerly occupied by the monks, faced south. The park seemed to have about forty acres. Near the house lay a succession of green meadows, charmingly crossed by several clear rivulets, with here and there a piece of water naturally placed without the least apparent artifice. Trees of elegant shape and varied foliage were distributed about. Grottos, cleverly managed, and massive terraces with dilapidated steps and rusty railings, gave a peculiar character to this lone retreat. Art had harmonized her constructions with the picturesque effects of nature. Human passions seemed to die at the feet of those great trees, which guarded this asylum from the tumult of the world as they shaded it from the fires of the sun.

"How desolate!" thought Monsieur d'Albon, observing the sombre expression which the ancient building gave to the landscape, gloomy as though a curse were on it. It seemed a fatal spot deserted by man. Ivy had stretched its tortuous muscles, covered by its rich green mantle, everywhere. Brown or green, red or yellow mosses and lichen spread their romantic tints on trees and seats and roofs and stones. The crumbling window-casings were hollowed by rain, defaced by time; the balconies were broken, the terraces demolished. Some of the outside shutters hung from a single hinge. The rotten doors seemed quite unable to resist an assailant. Covered with shining tufts of mistletoe, the branches of the neglected fruit-trees gave no sign of fruit. Grass grew in the paths. Such ruin and desolation cast a weird poesy on the scene, filling the souls of the spectators with dreamy thoughts. A poet would have stood there long, plunged in a melancholy reverie, admiring this disorder so full of harmony, this destruction which was not without its grace. Suddenly, the brown tiles shone, the mosses glittered, fantastic shadows danced upon the meadows and beneath the trees; fading colors revived; striking contrasts developed, the foliage of the trees and shrubs defined itself more clearly in the light. Then—the light went out. The landscape seemed to have spoken, and now was silent, returning to its gloom, or rather to the soft sad tones of an autumnal twilight.

"It is the palace of the Sleeping Beauty," said the marquis, beginning to view the house with the eyes of a land owner. "I wonder to whom it belongs! He must be a stupid fellow not to live in such an exquisite spot."

At that instant a woman sprang from beneath a chestnut-tree standing to the right of the gate, and, without making any noise, passed before the marquis as rapidly as the shadow of a cloud. This vision made him mute with surprise.

"Why, Albon, what's the matter?" asked the colonel.

"I am rubbing my eyes to know if I am asleep or awake," replied the marquis, with his face close to the iron rails as he tried to get another sight of the phantom.

"She must be beneath that fig-tree," he said, pointing to the foliage of a tree which rose above the wall to the left of the gate.

"She! who?"

"How can I tell?" replied Monsieur d'Albon. "A strange woman rose up there, just before me," he said in a low voice; "she seemed to come from the world of shades rather than from the land of the living. She is so slender, so light, so filmy, she must be diaphanous. Her face was as white as milk; her eyes, her clothes, her hair jet black. She looked at me as she flitted by, and though I may say I'm no coward, that cold immovable look froze the blood in my veins."

"Is she pretty?" asked Philippe.

"I don't know. I could see nothing but the eyes in that face."

"Well, let the dinner at Cassan go to the devil!" cried the colonel. "Suppose we stay here. I have a sudden childish desire to enter that singular house. Do you see those window-frames painted red, and the red lines on the doors and shutters? Doesn't the place look to you as if it belonged to the devil? — perhaps he inherited it from the monks. Come, let us pursue the black and white lady — forward, march!" cried Philippe, with forced gaiety.

At that instant the two huntsmen heard a cry that was something like that of a mouse caught in a trap. They listened. The rustle of a few shrubs sounded in the silence like the murmur of a breaking wave. In vain they listened for other sounds; the earth was dumb, and kept the secret of those light steps, if, indeed, the unknown woman moved at all.

"It is very singular!" said Philippe, as they skirted the park wall.

The two friends presently reached a path in the forest which led to the village of Chauvry. After following this path some way toward the main road to Paris, they came to another iron gate which led to the principal facade of the mysterious dwelling. On this side the dilapidation and disorder of the premises had reached their height. Immense cracks furrowed the walls of the house, which was built on three sides of a square. Fragments of tiles and slates lying on the ground, and the dilapidated condition of the roofs, were evidence of a total want of care on the part of the owners. The fruit had fallen from the trees and lay rotting on the ground; a cow was feeding on the lawn and treading down the flowers in the borders, while a goat browsed on the shoots of the vines and munched the unripe grapes.

"Here all is harmony; the devastation seems organized," said the colonel, pulling the chain of a bell; but the bell was without a clapper.

The huntsmen heard nothing but the curiously sharp noise of a rusty spring. Though very dilapidated, a little door made in the wall beside the iron gates resisted all their efforts to open it.

"Well, well, this is getting to be exciting," said de Sucy to his companion.

"If I were not a magistrate," replied Monsieur d'Albon, "I should think that woman was a witch."

As he said the words, the cow came to the iron gate and pushed her warm muzzle towards them, as if she felt the need of seeing human beings. Then a woman, if that name could be applied to the indefinable being who suddenly issued from a clump of bushes, pulled away the cow by its rope. This woman wore on her head a red handkerchief, beneath which trailed long locks of hair in color and shape like the flax on a distaff. She wore no fichu. A coarse woollen petticoat in black and gray stripes, too short by several inches, exposed her legs. She might have belonged to some tribe of Red-Skins described by Cooper, for her legs, neck, and arms were the color of brick. No ray of intelligence enlivened her vacant face. A few whitish hairs served her for eyebrows; the eyes themselves, of a dull blue, were cold and wan; and her mouth was so formed as to show the teeth, which were crooked, but as white as those of a dog.

"Here, my good woman!" called Monsieur de Sucy.

She came very slowly to the gate, looking with a silly expression at the two huntsmen, the sight of whom brought a forced and painful smile to her face.

"Where are we? Whose house is this? Who are you? Do you belong here?"

To these questions and several others which the two friends alternately addressed to her, she answered only with guttural sounds that seemed more like the growl of an animal than the voice of a human being.

"She must be deaf and dumb," said the marquis.

"Bons-Hommes!" cried the peasant woman.

"Ah! I see. This is, no doubt, the old monastery of the Bons-Hommes," said the marquis.

He renewed his questions. But, like a capricious child, the peasant woman colored, played with her wooden shoe, twisted the rope of the cow, which was now feeding peaceably, and looked at the two hunters, examining every part of their clothing; then she yelped, growled, and clucked, but did not speak.

"What is your name?" said Philippe, looking at her fixedly, as if he meant to mesmerize her.

"Genevieve," she said, laughing with a silly air.

"The cow is the most intelligent being we have seen so far," said the marquis. "I shall fire my gun and see if that will being some one."

Just as d'Albon raised his gun, the colonel stopped him with a gesture, and pointed to the form of a woman, probably the one who had so keenly piqued his curiosity. At this moment she seemed lost in the deepest meditation, and was coming with slow steps along a distant pathway, so that the two friends had ample time to examine her.

She was dressed in a ragged gown of black satin. Her long hair fell in masses of curls over her forehead, around her shoulders, and below her waist, serving her for a shawl. Accustomed no doubt to this disorder, she seldom pushed her hair from her forehead; and when she did so, it was with a sudden toss of her head which only for a moment cleared her forehead and eyes from the thick veil. Her gesture, like that of an animal, had a remarkable mechanical precision, the quickness of which seemed wonderful in a woman. The huntsmen were amazed to see her suddenly leap up on the branch of an apple-tree, and sit there with the ease of a bird. She gathered an apple and ate it; then she dropped to the ground with the graceful ease we admire in a squirrel. Her limbs possessed an elasticity which took from every movement the slightest appearance of effort or constraint. She played upon the turf, rolling herself about like a child; then, suddenly, she flung her feet and hands forward, and lay at full length on the grass, with the grace and natural ease of a young cat asleep in the sun. Thunder sounded in the distance, and she turned suddenly, rising on her hands and knees with the rapidity of a dog which hears a coming footstep.

The effects of this singular attitude was to separate into two heavy masses the volume of her black hair, which now fell on either side of her head, and allowed the two spectators to admire the white shoulders glistening like daisies in a field, and the throat, the perfection of which allowed them to judge of the other beauties of her figure.

Suddenly she uttered a distressful cry and rose to her feet. Her movements succeeded each other with such airiness and grace that she seemed not a creature of this world but a daughter of the atmosphere, as sung in the poems of Ossian. She ran toward a piece of water, shook one of her legs lightly to cast off her shoe, and began to dabble her foot, white as alabaster, in the current, admiring, perhaps, the undulations she thus produced upon the surface of the water. Then she knelt down at the edge of the stream and amused herself, like a child, in casting in her long tresses and pulling them abruptly out, to watch the shower of drops that glittered down, looking, as the sunlight struck athwart them, like a chaplet of pearls.

"That woman is mad!" cried the marquis.

A hoarse cry, uttered by Genevieve, seemed uttered as a warning to the unknown woman, who turned suddenly, throwing back her hair from either side of her face. At this instant the colonel and Monsieur d'Albon could distinctly see her features; she, herself, perceiving the two friends, sprang to the iron railing with the lightness and rapidity of a deer.

"Adieu!" she said, in a soft, harmonious voice, the melody of which did not convey the slightest feeling or the slightest thought.

Monsieur d'Albon admired the long lashes of her eyelids, the blackness of her eyebrows, and the dazzling whiteness of a skin devoid of even the faintest tinge of color. Tiny blue veins alone broke the uniformity of its pure white tones. When the marquis turned to his friend as if to share with him his amazement at the sight of this singular creature, he found him stretched on the ground as if dead. D'Albon fired his gun in the air to summon assistance, crying out "Help! help!" and then endeavored to revive the colonel. At the sound of the shot, the unknown woman, who had hitherto stood motionless, fled away with the rapidity of an arrow, uttering cries of fear like a wounded animal, and running hither and thither about the meadow with every sign of the greatest terror.

Monsieur d'Albon, hearing the rumbling of a carriage on the high-road to Ile-Adam, waved his handkerchief and shouted to its occupants for assistance. The carriage was immediately driven up to the old monastery, and the marquis recognized his neighbors, Monsieur and Madame de Granville, who at once gave up their carriage to the service of the two gentlemen. Madame de Granville had with her, by chance, a bottle of salts, which revived the colonel for a moment. When he opened his eyes he turned them to the meadow, where the unknown woman was still running and uttering her distressing cries. A smothered exclamation escaped him, which seemed to express a sense of horror; then he closed his eyes again, and made a gesture as if to implore his friend to remove him from that sight.

Monsieur and Madame de Granville placed their carriage entirely at the disposal of the marquis, assuring him courteously that they would like to continue their way on foot.

"Who is that lady?" asked the marquis, signing toward the unknown woman.

"I believe she comes from Moulins," replied Monsieur de Granville. "She is the Comtesse de Vandieres, and they say she is mad; but as she has only been here two months I will not vouch for the truth of these hearsays."

Monsieur d'Albon thanked his friends, and placing the colonel in the carriage, started with him for Cassan.

"It is she!" cried Philippe, recovering his senses.

"Who is she?" asked d'Albon.

"Stephanie. Ah, dead and living, living and mad! I fancied I was dying."

The prudent marquis, appreciating the gravity of the crisis through which his friend was passing, was careful not to question or excite him; he was only anxious to reach the chateau, for the change which had taken place in the colonel's features, in fact in his whole person, made him fear for his friend's reason. As soon, therefore, as the carriage had reached the main street of Ile-Adam, he dispatched the footman to the village doctor, so that the colonel was no sooner fairly in his bed at the chateau than the physician was beside him.

"If monsieur had not been many hours without food the shock would have killed him," said the doctor.

After naming the first precautions, the doctor left the room, to prepare, himself, a calming potion. The next day, Monsieur de Sucy was better, but the doctor still watched him carefully.

"I will admit to you, monsieur le marquis," he said, "that I have feared some affection of the brain. Monsieur de Sucy has received a violent shock; his passions are strong; but, in him, the first blow decides all. To-morrow he may be entirely out of danger."

The doctor was not mistaken; and the following day he allowed the marquis to see his friend.

"My dear d'Albon," said Philippe, pressing his hand, "I am going to ask a kindness of you. Go to the Bons-Hommes, and find out all you can of the lady we saw there; and return to me as quickly as you can; I shall count the minutes."

Monsieur d'Albon mounted his horse at once, and galloped to the old abbey. When he arrived there, he saw before the iron gate a tall, spare man with a very kindly face, who answered in the affirmative when asked if he lived there. Monsieur d'Albon then informed him of the reasons for his visit.

"What! monsieur," said the other, "was it you who fired that fatal shot? You very nearly killed my poor patient."

"But, monsieur, I fired in the air."

"You would have done the countess less harm had you fired at her."

"Then we must not reproach each other, monsieur, for the sight of the countess has almost killed my friend, Monsieur de Sucy."

"Heavens! can you mean Baron Philippe de Sucy?" cried the doctor, clasping his hands. "Did he go to Russia; was he at the passage of the Beresina?"

"Yes," replied d'Albon, "he was captured by the Cossacks and kept for five years in Siberia; he recovered his liberty a few months ago."

"Come in, monsieur," said the master of the house, leading the marquis into a room on the lower floor where everything bore the marks of capricious destruction. The silken curtains beside the windows were torn, while those of muslin remained intact.

"You see," said the tall old man, as they entered, "the ravages committed by that dear creature, to whom I devote myself. She is my niece; in spite of the impotence of my art, I hope some day to restore her reason by attempting a method which can only be employed, unfortunately, by very rich people."

Then, like all persons living in solitude who are afflicted with an ever present and ever renewed grief, he related to the marquis at length the following narrative, which is here condensed, and relieved of the many digressions made by both the narrator and the listener.

CHAPTER II.

THE PASSAGE OF THE BERESINA

Marechal Victor, when he started, about nine at night, from the heights of Studzianka, which he had defended, as the rear-guard of the retreating army, during the whole day of November 28th, 1812, left a thousand men behind him, with orders to protect to the last possible moment whichever of the two bridges across the Beresina might still exist. This rear-guard had devoted itself to the task of saving a frightful multitude of stragglers overcome by the cold, who obstinately refused to leave the bivouacs of the army. The heroism of this generous troop proved useless. The stragglers who flocked in masses to the banks of the Beresina found there, unhappily, an immense number of carriages, caissons, and articles of all kinds which the army had been forced to abandon when effecting its passage of the river on the 27th and 28th of November. Heirs to such unlooked-for riches, the unfortunate men, stupid with cold, took up their abode in the deserted bivouacs, broke up the material which they found there to build themselves cabins, made fuel of everything that came to hand, cut up the frozen carcasses of the horses for food, tore the cloth and the curtains from the carriages for coverlets, and went to sleep, instead of continuing their way and crossing quietly during the night that cruel Beresina, which an incredible fatality had already made so destructive to the army.

The apathy of these poor soldiers can only be conceived by those who remember to have crossed vast deserts of snow without other perspective than a snow horizon, without other drink than snow, without other bed than snow, without other food than snow or a few frozen beet-roots, a few handfuls of flour, or a little horseflesh. Dying of hunger, thirst, fatigue, and want of sleep, these unfortunates reached a shore where they saw before them wood, provisions, innumerable camp equipages, and carriages,—in short a whole town at their service. The village of Studzianka had been wholly taken to pieces and conveyed from the heights on which it stood to the plain. However forlorn and dangerous that refuge might be, its miseries and its perils only courted men who had lately seen nothing before them but the awful deserts of Russia. It was, in fact, a vast asylum which had an existence of twenty-four hours only.

Utter lassitude, and the sense of unexpected comfort, made that mass of men inaccessible to every thought but that of rest. Though the artillery of the left wing of the Russians kept up a steady fire on this mass,—visible like a stain now black, now flaming, in the midst of the trackless snow,—this shot and shell seemed to the torpid creatures only one inconvenience the more. It was like a thunderstorm, despised by all because the lightning strikes so few; the balls struck only here and there, the dying, the sick, the dead sometimes! Stragglers arrived in groups continually; but once here those perambulating corpses separated; each begged for himself a place near a fire; repulsed repeatedly, they met again, to obtain by force the hospitality already refused to them. Deaf to the voice of some of their officers, who warned them of probable destruction on the morrow, they spent the amount of courage necessary to cross the river in building that asylum of a night, in making one meal that they themselves doomed to be their last. The death that awaited them they considered no evil, provided they could have that one night's sleep. They thought nothing evil but hunger, thirst, and cold. When there was no more wood or food or fire, horrible struggles took place between fresh-comers and the rich who possessed a shelter. The weakest succumbed.

At last there came a moment when a number, pursued by the Russians, found only snow on which to bivouac, and these lay down to rise no more. Insensibly this mass of almost annihilated beings became so compact, so deaf, so torpid, so happy perhaps, that Marechal Victor, who had been their heroic defender by holding twenty thousand Russians under Wittgenstein at bay, was forced to open a passage by main force through this forest of men in order to cross the Beresina with five thousand gallant fellows whom he was taking to the emperor. The unfortunate malingerers allowed themselves to be crushed rather than stir; they perished in silence, smiling at their extinguished fires, without a thought of France.

It was not until ten o'clock that night that Marechal Victor reached the bank of the river. Before crossing the bridge which led to Zembin, he confided the fate of his own rear-guard now left in Studzianka to Eble, the savior of all those who survived the calamities of the Beresina. It was towards midnight when this great general, followed by one brave officer, left the cabin he occupied near the bridge, and studied the spectacle of that improvised camp placed between the bank of the river and Studzianka. The Russian cannon had ceased to thunder. Innumerable fires, which, amid that trackless waste of snow, burned pale and scarcely sent out any gleams, illumined here and there by sudden flashes forms and faces that were barely human. Thirty thousand poor wretches, belonging to all nations, from whom Napoleon had recruited his Russian army, were trifling away their lives with brutish indifference.

"Let us save them!" said General Eble to the officer who accompanied him. "To-morrow morning the Russians will be masters of Studzianka. We must burn the bridge the moment they appear. Therefore, my friend, take your courage in your hand! Go to the heights. Tell General Fournier he has barely time to evacuate his position, force a way through this crowd, and cross the bridge. When you have seen him in motion follow him. Find men you can trust, and the moment Fournier had crossed the bridge, burn, without pity, huts, equipages, caissons, carriages,— EVERYTHING! Drive that mass of men to the bridge. Compel all that has two legs to get to the other side of the river. The burning of everything—EVERYTHING—is now our last resource. If Berthier had let me destroy those damned camp equipages, this river would swallow only my poor pontoniers, those fifty heroes who will save the army, but who themselves will be forgotten."

The general laid his hand on his forehead and was silent. He felt that Poland would be his grave, and that no voice would rise to do justice to those noble men who stood in the water, the icy water of Beresina, to destroy the buttresses of the bridges. One alone of those heroes still lives—or, to speak more correctly, suffers—in a village, totally ignored.

The aide-de-camp started. Hardly had this generous officer gone a hundred yards towards Studzianka than General Eble wakened a number of his weary pontoniers, and began the work,—the charitable work of burning the bivouacs set up about the bridge, and forcing the sleepers, thus dislodged, to cross the river.

Meanwhile the young aide-de-camp reached, not without difficulty, the only wooden house still left standing in Studzianka.

"This barrack seems pretty full, comrade," he said to a man whom he saw by the doorway.

"If you can get in you'll be a clever trooper," replied the officer, without turning his head or ceasing to slice off with his sabre the bark of the logs of which the house was built.

"Is that you, Philippe?" said the aide-de-camp, recognizing a friend by the tones of his voice.

"Yes. Ha, ha! is it you, old fellow?" replied Monsieur de Sucy, looking at the aide-de-camp, who, like himself, was only twenty-three years of age. "I thought you were the other side of that cursed river. What are you here for? Have you brought cakes and wine for our dessert? You'll be welcome," and he went on slicing off the bark, which he gave as a sort of provender to his horse.

"I am looking for your commander to tell him, from General Eble, to make for Zembin. You'll have barely enough time to get through that crowd of men below. I am going presently to set fire to their camp and force them to march."

"You warm me up—almost! That news makes me perspire. I have two friends I MUST save. Ah! without those two to cling to me, I should be dead already. It is for them that I feed my horse and don't eat myself. Have you any food,—a mere crust? It is thirty hours since anything has gone into my stomach, and yet I have fought like a madman—just to keep a little warmth and courage in me."

"Poor Philippe, I have nothing—nothing! But where's your general,—in this house?"

"No, don't go there; the place is full of wounded. Go up the street; you'll find on your left a sort of pig-pen; the general is there. Good-bye, old fellow. If we ever dance a trenis on a Paris floor—"

He did not end his sentence; the north wind blew at that moment with such ferocity that the aide-de-camp hurried on to escape being frozen, and the lips of Major de Sucy stiffened. Silence reigned, broken only by the moans which came from the house, and the dull sound made by the major's horse as it chewed in a fury of hunger the icy bark of the trees with which the house was built. Monsieur de Sucy replaced his sabre in its scabbard, took the bridle of the precious horse he had hitherto been able to preserve, and led it, in spite of the animal's resistance, from the wretched fodder it appeared to think excellent.

"We'll start, Bichette, we'll start! There's none but you, my beauty, who can save Stephanie. Ha! by and bye you and I may be able to rest—and die," he added.

Philippe, wrapped in a fur pelisse, to which he owed his preservation and his energy, began to run, striking his feet hard upon the frozen snow to keep them warm. Scarcely had he gone a few hundred yards from the village than he saw a blaze in the direction of the place where, since morning, he had left his carriage in charge of his former orderly, an old soldier. Horrible anxiety laid hold of him. Like all others who were controlled during this fatal retreat by some powerful sentiment, he found a strength to save his friends which he could not have put forth to save himself.

Presently he reached a slight declivity at the foot of which, in a spot sheltered from the enemy's balls, he had stationed the carriage, containing a young woman, the companion of his childhood, the being most dear to him on earth. At a few steps distant from the vehicle he now found a company of some thirty stragglers collected around an immense fire, which they were feeding with planks, caisson covers, wheels, and broken carriages. These soldiers were, no doubt, the last comers of that crowd who, from the base of the hill of Studzianka to the fatal river, formed an ocean of heads intermingled with fires and huts,—a living sea, swayed by motions that were almost imperceptible, and giving forth a murmuring sound that rose at times to frightful outbursts. Driven by famine and despair, these poor wretches must have rifled the carriage before de Sucy reached it. The old general and his young wife, whom he had left lying in piles of clothes and wrapped in mantles and pelisses, were now on the snow, crouching before the fire. One door of the carriage was already torn off.

No sooner did the men about the fire hear the tread of the major's horse than a hoarse cry, the cry of famine, arose,—

"A horse! a horse!"

Those voices formed but one voice.

"Back! back! look out for yourself!" cried two or three soldiers, aiming at the mare. Philippe threw himself before his animal, crying out,—

"You villains! I'll throw you into your own fire. There are plenty of dead horses up there. Go and fetch them."

"Isn't he a joker, that officer! One, two—get out of the way," cried a colossal grenadier. "No, you won't, hey! Well, as you please, then."

A woman's cry rose higher than the report of the musket. Philippe fortunately was not touched, but Bichette, mortally wounded, was struggling in the throes of death. Three men darted forward and dispatched her with their bayonets.

"Cannibals!" cried Philippe, "let me at any rate take the horse-cloth and my pistols."

"Pistols, yes," replied the grenadier. "But as for that horse-cloth, no! here's a poor fellow afoot, with nothing in his stomach for two days, and shivering in his rags. It is our general."

Philippe kept silence as he looked at the man, whose boots were worn out, his trousers torn in a dozen places, while nothing but a ragged fatigue-cap covered with ice was on his head. He hastened, however, to take his pistols. Five men dragged the mare to the fire, and cut her up with the dexterity of a Parisian butcher. The pieces were instantly seized and flung upon the embers.

The major went up to the young woman, who had uttered a cry on recognizing him. He found her motionless, seated on a cushion beside the fire. She looked at him silently, without smiling. Philippe then saw the soldier to whom he had confided the carriage; the man was wounded. Overcome by numbers, he had been forced to yield to the malingerers who attacked him; and, like the dog who defended to the last possible moment his master's dinner, he had taken his share of the booty, and was now sitting beside the fire, wrapped in a white sheet by way of cloak, and turning carefully on the embers a slice of the mare. Philippe saw upon his face the joy these preparations gave him. The Comte de Vandieres, who, for the last few days, had fallen into a state of second childhood, was seated on a cushion beside his wife, looking fixedly at the fire, which was beginning to thaw his torpid limbs. He had shown no emotion of any kind, either at Philippe's danger, or at the fight which ended in the pillage of the carriage and their expulsion from it.

At first de Sucy took the hand of the young countess, as if to show her his affection, and the grief he felt at seeing her reduced to such utter misery; then he grew silent; seated beside her on a heap of snow which was turning into a rivulet as it melted, he yielded himself up to the happiness of being warm, forgetting their peril, forgetting all things. His face assumed, in spite of himself, an expression of almost stupid joy, and he waited with impatience until the fragment of the mare given to his orderly was cooked. The smell of the roasting flesh increased his hunger, and his hunger silenced his heart, his courage, and his love. He looked, without anger, at the results of the pillage of his carriage. All the men seated around the fire had shared his blankets, cushions, pelisses, robes, also the clothing of the Comte and Comtesse de Vandieres and his own. Philippe looked about him to see if there was anything left in or near the vehicle that was worth saving. By the light of the flames he saw gold and diamonds and plate scattered everywhere, no one having thought it worth his while to take any.

Each of the individuals collected by chance around this fire maintained a silence that was almost horrible, and did nothing but what he judged necessary for his own welfare. Their misery was even grotesque. Faces, discolored by cold, were covered with a layer of mud, on which tears had made a furrow from the eyes to the beard, showing the thickness of that miry mask. The filth of their long beards made these men still more repulsive. Some were wrapped in the countess's shawls, others wore the trappings of horses and muddy saddlecloths, or masses of rags from which the hoar-frost hung; some had a boot on one leg and a shoe on the other; in fact, there were none whose costume did not present some laughable singularity. But in presence of such amusing sights the men themselves were grave and gloomy. The silence was broken only by the snapping of the wood, the crackling of the flames, the distant murmur of the camps, and the blows of the sabre given to what remained of Bichette in search of her tenderest morsels. A few miserable creatures, perhaps more weary than the rest, were sleeping; when one of their number rolled into the fire no one attempted to help him out. These stern logicians argued that if he were not dead his burns would warn him to find a safer place. If the poor wretch waked in the flames and perished, no one cared. Two or three soldiers looked at each other to justify their own indifference by that of others. Twice this scene had taken place before the eyes of the countess, who said nothing. When the various pieces of Bichette, placed here and there upon the embers, were sufficiently broiled, each man satisfied his hunger with the gluttony that disgusts us when we see it in animals.

"This is the first time I ever saw thirty infantrymen on one horse," cried the grenadier who had shot the mare.

It was the only jest made that night which proved the national character.

Soon the great number of these poor soldiers wrapped themselves in what they could find and lay down on planks, or whatever would keep them from contact with the snow, and slept, heedless of the morrow. When the major was warm, and his hunger appeased, an invincible desire to sleep weighed down his eyelids. During the short moment of his struggle against that desire he looked at the young woman, who had turned her face to the fire and was now asleep, leaving her closed eyes and a portion of her forehead exposed to sight. She was wrapped in a furred pelisse and a heavy dragoon's cloak; her head rested on a pillow stained with blood; an astrakhan hood, kept in place by a handkerchief knotted round her neck, preserved her face from the cold as much as possible. Her feet were wrapped in the cloak. Thus rolled into a bundle, as it were, she looked like nothing at all. Was she the last of the "vivandieres"? Was she a charming woman, the glory of a lover, the queen of Parisian salons? Alas! even the eye of her most devoted friend could trace no sign of anything feminine in that mass of rags and tatters. Love had succumbed to cold in the heart of a woman!

Through the thick veils of irresistible sleep, the major soon saw the husband and wife as mere points or formless objects. The flames of the fire, those outstretched figures, the relentless cold, waiting, not three feet distant from that fugitive heat, became all a dream. One importunate thought terrified Philippe:

"If I sleep, we shall all die; I will not sleep," he said to himself.

And yet he slept.

A terrible clamor and an explosion awoke him an hour later. The sense of his duty, the peril of his friend, fell suddenly on his heart. He uttered a cry that was like a roar. He and his orderly were alone afoot. A sea of fire lay before them in the darkness of the night, licking up the cabins and the bivouacs; cries of despair, howls, and imprecations reached their ears; they saw against the flames thousands of human beings with agonized or furious faces. In the midst of that hell, a column of soldiers was forcing its way to the bridge, between two hedges of dead bodies.

"It is the retreat of the rear-guard!" cried the major. "All hope is gone!"

"I have saved your carriage, Philippe," said a friendly voice.

Turning round, de Sucy recognized the young aide-de-camp in the flaring of the flames.

"Ah! all is lost!" replied the major, "they have eaten my horse; and how can I make this stupid general and his wife walk?"

"Take a brand from the fire and threaten them."

"Threaten the countess!"

"Good-bye," said the aide-de-camp, "I have scarcely time to get across that fatal river—and I MUST; I have a mother in France. What a night! These poor wretches prefer to lie here in the snow; half will allow themselves to perish in those flames rather than rise and move on. It is four o'clock, Philippe! In two hours the Russians will begin to move. I assure you you will again see the Beresina choked with corpses. Philippe! think of yourself! You have no horses, you cannot carry the countess in your arms. Come—come with me!" he said urgently, pulling de Sucy by the arm.

"My friend! abandon Stephanie!"

De Sucy seized the countess, made her stand upright, shook her with the roughness of a despairing man, and compelled her to wake up. She looked at him with fixed, dead eyes.

"You must walk, Stephanie, or we shall all die here."

For all answer the countess tried to drop again upon the snow and sleep. The aide-de-camp seized a brand from the fire and waved it in her face.

"We will save her in spite of herself!" cried Philippe, lifting the countess and placing her in the carriage.

He returned to implore the help of his friend. Together they lifted the old general, without knowing whether he were dead or alive, and put him beside his wife. The major then rolled over the men who were sleeping on his blankets, which he tossed into the carriage, together with some roasted fragments of his mare.

"What do you mean to do?" asked the aide-de-camp.

"Drag them."

"You are crazy."

"True," said Philippe, crossing his arms in despair.

Suddenly, he was seized by a last despairing thought.

"To you," he said, grasping the sound arm of his orderly, "I confide her for one hour. Remember that you must die sooner than let any one approach her."

The major then snatched up the countess's diamonds, held them in one hand, drew his sabre with the other, and began to strike with the flat of its blade such of the sleepers as he thought the most intrepid. He succeeded in awaking the colossal grenadier, and two other men whose rank it was impossible to tell.

"We are done for!" he said.

"I know it," said the grenadier, "but I don't care."

"Well, death for death, wouldn't you rather sell your life for a pretty woman, and take your chances of seeing France?"

"I'd rather sleep," said a man, rolling over on the snow, "and if you trouble me again, I'll stick my bayonet into your stomach."

"What is the business, my colonel?" said the grenadier. "That man is drunk; he's a Parisian; he likes his ease."

"That is yours, my brave grenadier," cried the major, offering him a string of diamonds, "if you will follow me and fight like a madman. The Russians are ten minutes' march from here; they have horses; we are going up to their first battery for a pair."

"But the sentinels?"

"One of us three—" he interrupted himself, and turned to the aide-de-camp. "You will come, Hippolyte, won't you?"

Hippolyte nodded.

"One of us," continued the major, "will take care of the sentinel. Besides, perhaps they are asleep too, those cursed Russians."

"Forward! major, you're a brave one! But you'll give me a lift on your carriage?" said the grenadier.

"Yes, if you don't leave your skin up there—If I fall, Hippolyte, and you, grenadier, promise me to do your utmost to save the countess."

"Agreed!" cried the grenadier.

They started for the Russian lines, toward one of the batteries which had so decimated the hapless wretches lying on the banks of the river. A few moments later, the gallop of two horses echoed over the snow, and the wakened artillery men poured out a volley which ranged above the heads of the sleeping men. The pace of the horses was so fleet that their steps resounded like the blows of a blacksmith on his anvil. The generous aide-de-camp was killed. The athletic grenadier was safe and sound. Philippe in defending Hippolyte had received a bayonet in his shoulder; but he clung to his horse's mane, and clasped him so tightly with his knees that the animal was held as in a vice.

"God be praised!" cried the major, finding his orderly untouched, and the carriage in its place.

"If you are just, my officer, you will get me the cross for this," said the man. "We've played a fine game of guns and sabres here, I can tell you."

"We have done nothing yet—Harness the horses. Take these ropes."

"They are not long enough."

"Grenadier, turn over those sleepers, and take their shawls and linen, to eke out."

"Tiens! that's one dead," said the grenadier, stripping the first man he came to. "Bless me! what a joke, they are all dead!"

"All?"

"Yes, all; seems as if horse-meat must be indigestible if eaten with snow."

The words made Philippe tremble. The cold was increasing.

"My God! to lose the woman I have saved a dozen times!"

The major shook the countess.

"Stephanie! Stephanie!"

The young woman opened her eyes.

"Madame! we are saved."

"Saved!" she repeated, sinking down again.

The horses were harnessed as best they could. The major, holding his sabre in his well hand, with his pistols in his belt, gathered up the reins with the other hand and mounted one horse while the grenadier mounted the other. The orderly, whose feet were frozen, was thrown inside the carriage, across the general and the countess. Excited by pricks from a sabre, the horses drew the carriage rapidly, with a sort of fury, to the plain, where innumerable obstacles awaited it. It was impossible to force a way without danger of crushing the sleeping men, women, and even children, who refused to move when the grenadier awoke them. In vain did Monsieur de Sucy endeavor to find the swathe cut by the rear-guard through the mass of human beings; it was already obliterated, like the wake of a vessel through the sea. They could only creep along, being often stopped by soldiers who threatened to kill their horses.

"Do you want to reach the bridge?" said the grenadier.

"At the cost of my life—at the cost of the whole world!"

"Then forward, march! you can't make omelets without breaking eggs."

And the grenadier of the guard urged the horses over men and bivouacs with bloody wheels and a double line of corpses on either side of them. We must do him the justice to say that he never spared his breath in shouting in stentorian tones,—

"Look out there, carrion!"

"Poor wretches!" cried the major.

"Pooh! that or the cold, that or the cannon," said the grenadier, prodding the horses, and urging them on.

A catastrophe, which might well have happened to them much sooner, put a stop to their advance. The carriage was overturned.

"I expected it," cried the imperturbable grenadier. "Ho! ho! your man is dead."

"Poor Laurent!" said the major.

"Laurent? Was he in the 5th chasseurs?"

"Yes."

"Then he was my cousin. Oh, well, this dog's life isn't happy enough to waste any joy in grieving for him."

The carriage could not be raised; the horses were taken out with serious and, as it proved, irreparable loss of time. The shock of the overturn was so violent that the young countess, roused from her lethargy, threw off her coverings and rose.

"Philippe, where are we?" she cried in a gentle voice, looking about her.

"Only five hundred feet from the bridge. We are now going to cross the Beresina, Stephanie, and once across I will not torment you any more; you shall sleep; we shall be in safety, and can reach Wilna easily.—God grant that she may never know what her life has cost!" he thought.

"Philippe! you are wounded!"

"That is nothing."

Too late! the fatal hour had come. The Russian cannon sounded the reveille. Masters of Studzianka, they could sweep the plain, and by daylight the major could see two of their columns moving and forming on the heights. A cry of alarm arose from the multitude, who started to their feet in an instant. Every man now understood his danger instinctively, and the whole mass rushed to gain the bridge with the motion of a wave.

The Russians came down with the rapidity of a conflagration. Men, women, children, horses,—all rushed tumultuously to the bridge. Fortunately the major, who was carrying the countess, was still some distance from it. General Eble had just set fire to the supports on the other bank. In spite of the warnings shouted to those who were rushing upon the bridge, not a soul went back. Not only did the bridge go down crowded with human beings, but the impetuosity of that flood of men toward the fatal bank was so furious that a mass of humanity poured itself violently into the river like an avalanche. Not a cry was heard; the only sound was like the dropping of monstrous stones into the water. Then the Beresina was a mass of floating corpses.

The retrograde movement of those who now fell back into the plain to escape the death before them was so violent, and their concussion against those who were advancing from the rear so terrible, that numbers were smothered or trampled to death. The Comte and Comtesse de Vandieres owed their lives to their carriage, behind which Philippe forced them, using it as a breastwork. As for the major and the grenadier, they found their safety in their strength. They killed to escape being killed.

This hurricane of human beings, the flux and reflux of living bodies, had the effect of leaving for a few short moments the whole bank of the Beresina deserted. The multitude were surging to the plain. If a few men rushed to the river, it was less in the hope of reaching the other bank, which to them was France, than to rush from the horrors of Siberia. Despair proved an aegis to some bold hearts. One officer sprang from ice-cake to ice-cake, and reached the opposite shore. A soldier clambered miraculously over mounds of dead bodies and heaps of ice. The multitude finally comprehended that the Russians would not put to death a body of twenty thousand men, without arms, torpid, stupid, unable to defend themselves; and each man awaited his fate with horrible resignation. Then the major and the grenadier, the general and his wife, remained almost alone on the river bank, a few steps from the spot where the bridge had been. They stood there, with dry eyes, silent, surrounded by heaps of dead. A few sound soldiers, a few officers to whom the emergency had restored their natural energy, were near them. This group consisted of some fifty men in all. The major noticed at a distance of some two hundred yards the remains of another bridge intended for carriages and destroyed the day before.

"Let us make a raft!" he cried.

He had hardly uttered the words before the whole group rushed to the ruins, and began to pick up iron bolts, and screws, and pieces of wood and ropes, whatever materials they could find that were suitable for the construction of a raft. A score of soldiers and officers, who were armed, formed a guard, commanded by the major, to protect the workers against the desperate attacks which might be expected from the crowd, if their scheme was discovered. The instinct of freedom, strong in all prisoners, inspiring them to miraculous acts, can only be compared with that which now drove to action these unfortunate Frenchmen.

"The Russians! the Russians are coming!" cried the defenders to the workers; and the work went on, the raft increased in length and breadth and depth. Generals, soldiers, colonel, all put their shoulders to the wheel; it was a true image of the building of Noah's ark. The young countess, seated beside her husband, watched the progress of the work with regret that she could not help it; and yet she did assist in making knots to secure the cordage.

At last the raft was finished. Forty men launched it on the river, a dozen others holding the cords which moored it to the shore. But no sooner had the builders seen their handiwork afloat, than they sprang from the bank with odious selfishness. The major, fearing the fury of this first rush, held back the countess and the general, but too late he saw the whole raft covered, men pressing together like crowds at a theatre.

"Savages!" he cried, "it was I who gave you the idea of that raft. I have saved you, and you deny me a place."

A confused murmur answered him. The men at the edge of the raft, armed with long sticks, pressed with violence against the shore to send off the frail construction with sufficient impetus to force its way through corpses and ice-floes to the other shore.

"Thunder of heaven! I'll sweep you into the water if you don't take the major and his two companions," cried the stalwart grenadier, who swung his sabre, stopped the departure, and forced the men to stand closer in spite of furious outcries.

"I shall fall," — "I am falling," — "Push off! push off! — Forward!" resounded on all sides.

The major looked with haggard eyes at Stephanie, who lifted hers to heaven with a feeling of sublime resignation.

"To die with thee!" she said.

There was something even comical in the position of the men in possession of the raft. Though they were uttering awful groans and imprecations, they dared not resist the grenadier, for in truth they were so closely packed together, that a push to one man might send half of them overboard. This danger was so pressing that a cavalry captain endeavored to get rid of the grenadier; but the latter, seeing the hostile movement of the officer, seized him round the waist and flung him into the water, crying out, —

"Ha! ha! my duck, do you want to drink? Well, then, drink!—Here are two places," he cried. "Come, major, toss me the little woman and follow yourself. Leave that old fossil, who'll be dead by to-morrow."

"Make haste!" cried the voice of all, as one man.

"Come, major, they are grumbling, and they have a right to do so."

The Comte de Vandieres threw off his wrappings and showed himself in his general's uniform.

"Let us save the count," said Philippe.

Stephanie pressed his hand, and throwing herself on his breast, she clasped him tightly.

"Adieu!" she said.

They had understood each other.

The Comte de Vandieres recovered sufficient strength and presence of mind to spring upon the raft, whither Stephanie followed him, after turning a last look to Philippe.

"Major! will you take my place? I don't care a fig for life," cried the grenadier. "I've neither wife nor child nor mother."

"I confide them to your care," said the major, pointing to the count and his wife.

"Then be easy; I'll care for them, as though they were my very eyes."

The raft was now sent off with so much violence toward the opposite side of the river, that as it touched ground, the shock was felt by all. The count, who was at the edge of it, lost his balance and fell into the river; as he fell, a cake of sharp ice caught him, and cut off his head, flinging it to a great distance.

"See there! major!" cried the grenadier.

"Adieu!" said a woman's voice.

Philippe de Sucy fell to the ground, overcome with horror and fatigue.

CHAPTER III.

THE CURE

"My poor niece became insane," continued the physician, after a few moment's silence. "Ah! monsieur," he said, seizing the marquis's hand, "life has been awful indeed for that poor little woman, so young, so delicate! After being, by dreadful fatality, separated from the grenadier, whose name was Fleuriot, she was dragged about for two years at the heels of the army, the plaything of a crowd of wretches. She was often, they tell me, barefooted, and scarcely clothed; for months together, she had no care, no food but what she could pick up; sometimes kept in hospitals, sometimes driven away like an animal, God alone knows the horrors that poor unfortunate creature has survived. She was locked up in a madhouse, in a little town in Germany, at the time her relatives, thinking her dead, divided her property. In 1816, the grenadier Fleuriot was at an inn in Strasburg, where she went after making her escape from the madhouse. Several peasants told the grenadier that she had lived for a whole month in the forest, where they had tracked her in vain, trying to catch her, but she had always escaped them. I was then staying a few miles from Strasburg. Hearing much talk of a wild woman caught in the woods, I felt a desire to ascertain the truth of the ridiculous stories which were current about her. What were my feelings on beholding my own niece! Fleuriot told me all he knew of her dreadful history. I took the poor man with my niece back to my home in Auvergne, where, unfortunately, I lost him some months later. He had some slight control over Madame de Vandieres; he alone could induce her to wear clothing. 'Adieu,' that word, which is her only language, she seldom uttered at that time. Fleuriot had endeavored to awaken in her a few ideas, a few memories of the past; but he failed; all that he gained was to make her say that melancholy word a little oftener. Still, the grenadier knew how to amuse her and play with her; my hope was in him, but—"

He was silent for a moment.

"Here," he continued, "she has found another creature, with whom she seems to have some strange understanding. It is a poor idiotic peasant-girl, who, in spite of her ugliness and stupidity, loved a man, a mason. The mason was willing to marry her, as she had some property. Poor Genevieve was happy for a year; she dressed in her best to dance with her lover on Sunday; she comprehended love; in her heart and soul there was room for that one sentiment. But the mason, Dallot, reflected. He found a girl with all her senses, and more land than Genevieve, and he deserted the poor creature. Since then she has lost the little intellect that love developed in her; she can do nothing but watch the cows, or help at harvesting.

My niece and this poor girl are friends, apparently by some invisible chain of their common destiny, by the sentiment in each which has caused their madness. See!" added Stephanie's uncle, leading the marquis to a window.

The latter then saw the countess seated on the ground between Genevieve's legs. The peasant-girl, armed with a huge horn comb, was giving her whole attention to the work of disentangling the long black hair of the poor countess, who was uttering little stifled cries, expressive of some instinctive sense of pleasure. Monsieur d'Albon shuddered as he saw the utter abandonment of the body, the careless animal ease which revealed in the hapless woman a total absence of soul.

"Philippe, Philippe!" he muttered, "the past horrors are nothing!—Is there no hope?" he asked.

The old physician raised his eyes to heaven.

"Adieu, monsieur," said the marquis, pressing his hand. "My friend is expecting me. He will soon come to you."

"Then it was really she!" cried de Sucy at d'Albon's first words. "Ah! I still doubted it," he added, a few tears falling from his eyes, which were habitually stern.

"Yes, it is the Comtesse de Vandieres," replied the marquis.

The colonel rose abruptly from his bed and began to dress.

"Philippe!" cried his friend, "are you mad?"

"I am no longer ill," replied the colonel, simply. "This news has quieted my suffering. What pain can I feel when I think of Stephanie? I am going to the Bons-Hommes, to see her, speak to her, cure her. She is free. Well, happiness will smile upon us—or Providence is not in this world. Think you that that poor woman could hear my voice and not recover reason?"

"She has already seen you and not recognized you," said his friend, gently, for he felt the danger of Philippe's excited hopes, and tried to cast a salutary doubt upon them.

The colonel quivered; then he smiled, and made a motion of incredulity. No one dared to oppose his wish, and within a very short time he reached the old priory.

"Where is she?" he cried, on arriving.

"Hush!" said her uncle, "she is sleeping. See, here she is."

Philippe then saw the poor insane creature lying on a bench in the sun. Her head was protected from the heat by a forest of hair which fell in tangled locks over her face. Her arms hung gracefully to the ground; her body lay easily posed like that of a doe; her feet were folded under her without effort; her bosom rose and fell at regular intervals; her skin, her complexion, had that porcelain whiteness, which we admire so much in the clear transparent faces of children. Standing motionless beside her, Genevieve held in her hand a branch which Stephanie had doubtless climbed a tall poplar to obtain, and the poor idiot was gently waving it above her sleeping companion, to chase away the flies and cool the atmosphere.

The peasant-woman gazed at Monsieur Fanjat and the colonel; then, like an animal which recognizes its master, she turned her head slowly to the countess, and continued to watch her, without giving any sign of surprise or intelligence. The air was stifling; the stone bench glittered in the sunlight; the meadow exhaled to heaven those impish vapors which dance and dart above the herbage like silvery dust; but Genevieve seemed not to feel this all-consuming heat.

The colonel pressed the hand of the doctor violently in his own. Tears rolled from his eyes along his manly cheeks, and fell to the earth at the feet of his Stephanie.

"Monsieur," said the uncle, "for two years past, my heart is broken day by day. Soon you will be like me. You may not always weep, but you will always feel your sorrow."

The two men understood each other; and again, pressing each other's hands, they remained motionless, contemplating the exquisite calmness which sleep had cast upon that graceful creature. From time to time she gave a sigh, and that sigh, which had all the semblance of sensibilities, made the unhappy colonel tremble with hope.

"Alas!" said Monsieur Fanjat, "do not deceive yourself, monsieur; there is no meaning in her sigh."

Those who have ever watched for hours with delight the sleep of one who is tenderly beloved, whose eyes will smile to them at waking, can understand the sweet yet terrible emotion that shook the colonel's soul. To him, this sleep was an illusion; the waking might be death, death in its most awful form. Suddenly, a little goat jumped in three bounds to the bench, and smelt at Stephanie, who waked at the sound. She sprang to her feet, but so lightly that the movement did not frighten the freakish animal; then she caught sight of Philippe, and darted away, followed by her four-footed friend, to a hedge of elders; there she uttered the same little cry like a frightened bird, which the two men had heard near the other gate. Then she climbed an acacia, and nestling into its tufted top, she watched the stranger with the inquisitive attention of the forest birds.

"Adieu, adieu, adieu," she said, without the soul communicating one single intelligent inflexion to the word.

It was uttered impassively, as the bird sings his note.

"She does not recognize me!" cried the colonel, in despair. "Stephanie! it is Philippe, thy Philippe, PHILIPPE!"

And the poor soldier went to the acacia; but when he was a few steps from it, the countess looked at him, as if defying him, although a slight expression of fear seemed to flicker in her eye; then, with a single bound she sprang from the acacia to a laburnum, and thence to a Norway fir, where she darted from branch to branch with extraordinary agility.

"Do not pursue her," said Monsieur Fanjat to the colonel, "or you will arouse an aversion which might become insurmountable. I will help you to tame her and make her come to you. Let us sit on this bench. If you pay no attention to her, she will come of her own accord to examine you."

"SHE! not to know me! to flee me!" repeated the colonel, seating himself on a bench with his back to a tree that shaded it, and letting his head fall upon his breast.

The doctor said nothing. Presently, the countess came gently down the fir-tree, letting herself swing easily on the branches, as the wind swayed them. At each branch she stopped to examine the stranger; but seeing him motionless, she at last sprang to the ground and came slowly towards him across the grass. When she reached a tree about ten feet distant, against which she leaned, Monsieur Fan-jat said to the colonel in a low voice, —

"Take out, adroitly, from my right hand pocket some lumps of sugar you will feel there. Show them to her, and she will come to us. I will renounce in your favor my sole means of giving her pleasure. With sugar, which she passionately loves, you will accustom her to approach you, and to know you again."

"When she was a woman," said Philippe, sadly, "she had no taste for sweet things."

When the colonel showed her the lump of sugar, holding it between the thumb and forefinger of his right hand, she again uttered her little wild cry, and sprang toward him; then she stopped, struggling against the instinctive fear he caused her; she looked at the sugar and turned away her head alternately, precisely like a dog whose master forbids him to touch his food until he has said a letter of the alphabet which he slowly repeats. At last the animal desire triumphed over fear. Stephanie darted to Philippe, cautiously putting out her little brown hand to seize the prize, touched the fingers of her poor lover as she snatched the sugar, and fled away among the trees. This dreadful scene overcame the colonel; he burst into tears and rushed into the house.

"Has love less courage than friendship?" Monsieur Fanjat said to him. "I have some hope, Monsieur le baron. My poor niece was in a far worse state than that in which you now find her."

"How was that possible?" cried Philippe.

"She went naked," replied the doctor.

The colonel made a gesture of horror and turned pale. The doctor saw in that sudden pallor alarming symptoms; he felt the colonel's pulse, found him in a violent fever, and half persuaded, half compelled him to go to bed. Then he gave him a dose of opium to ensure a calm sleep.

Eight days elapsed, during which Colonel de Sucy struggled against mortal agony; tears no longer came to his eyes. His soul, often lacerated, could not harden itself to the sight of Stephanie's insanity; but he covenanted, so to speak, with his cruel situation, and found some assuaging of his sorrow. He had the courage to slowly tame the countess by bringing her sweetmeats; he took such pains in choosing them, and he learned so well how to keep the little conquests he sought to make upon her instincts—that last shred of her intellect—that he ended by making her much TAMER than she had ever been.

Every morning he went into the park, and if, after searching for her long, he could not discover on what tree she was swaying, nor the covert in which she crouched to play with a bird, nor the roof on which she might have clambered, he would whistle the well-known air of "Partant pour la Syrie," to which some tender memory of their love attached. Instantly, Stephanie would run to him with the lightness of a fawn. She was now so accustomed to see him, that he frightened her no longer. Soon she was willing to sit upon his knee, and clasp him closely with her thin and agile arm. In that attitude—so dear to lovers!—Philippe would feed her with sugarplums. Then, having eaten those that he gave her, she would often search his pockets with gestures that had all the mechanical velocity of a monkey's motions. When she was very sure there was nothing more, she looked at Philippe with clear eyes, without ideas, with recognition. Then she would play with him, trying at times to take off his boots to see his feet, tearing his gloves, putting on his hat; she would even let him pass his hands through her hair, and take her in his arms; she accepted, but without pleasure, his ardent kisses. She would look at him silently, without emotion, when his tears flowed; but she always understood his "Partant pour la Syrie," when he whistled it, though he never succeeded in teaching her to say her own name Stephanie.

Philippe was sustained in his agonizing enterprise by hope, which never abandoned him. When, on fine autumn mornings, he found the countess sitting peacefully on a bench, beneath a poplar now yellowing, the poor lover would sit at her feet, looking into her eyes as long as she would let him, hoping ever that the light that was in them would become intelligent. Sometimes the thought deluded him that he saw those hard immovable rays softening, vibrating, living, and he cried out,—

"Stephanie! Stephanie! thou hearest me, thou seest me!"

But she listened to that cry as to a noise, the soughing of the wind in the tree-tops, or the lowing of the cow on the back of which she climbed. Then the colonel would wring his hands in despair,—despair that was new each day.

One evening, under a calm sky, amid the silence and peace of that rural haven, the doctor saw, from a distance, that the colonel was loading his pistols. The old man felt then that the young man had ceased to hope; he felt the blood rushing to his heart, and if he conquered the vertigo that threatened him, it was because he would rather see his niece living and mad than dead. He hastened up.

"What are you doing?" he said.

"That is for me," replied the colonel, pointing to a pistol already loaded, which was lying on the bench; "and this is for her," he added, as he forced the wad into the weapon he held.

The countess was lying on the ground beside him, playing with the balls.

"Then you do not know," said the doctor, coldly, concealing his terror, "that in her sleep last night she called you: Philippe!"

"She called me!" cried the baron, dropping his pistol, which Stephanie picked up. He took it from her hastily, caught up the one that was on the bench, and rushed away.

"Poor darling!" said the doctor, happy in the success of his lie. He pressed the poor creature to his breast, and continued speaking to himself: "He would have killed thee, selfish man! because he suffers. He does not love thee for thyself, my child! But we forgive, do we not? He is mad, out of his senses, but thou art only senseless. No, God alone should call thee to Him. We think thee unhappy, we pity thee because thou canst not share our sorrows, fools that we are!—But," he said, sitting down and taking her on his knee, "nothing troubles thee; thy life is like that of a bird, of a fawn—"

As he spoke she darted upon a young blackbird which was hopping near them, caught it with a little note of satisfaction, strangled it, looked at it, dead in her hand, and flung it down at the foot of a tree without a thought.

The next day, as soon as it was light, the colonel came down into the gardens, and looked about for Stephanie,—he believed in the coming happiness. Not finding her he whistled. When his darling came to him, he took her on his arm; they walked together thus for the first time, and he led her within a group of trees, the autumn foliage of which was dropping to the breeze. The colonel sat down. Of her own accord Stephanie placed herself on his knee. Philippe trembled with joy.

"Love," he said, kissing her hands passionately, "I am Philippe."

She looked at him with curiosity.

"Come," he said, pressing her to him, "dost thou feel my heart? It has beaten for thee alone. I love thee ever. Philippe is not dead; he is not dead, thou art on him, in his arms. Thou art MY Stephanie; I am thy Philippe."

"Adieu," she said, "adieu."

The colonel quivered, for he fancied he saw his own excitement communicated to his mistress. His heart-rending cry, drawn from him by despair, that last effort of an eternal love, of a delirious passion, was successful, the mind of his darling was awaking.

"Ah! Stephanie! Stephanie! we shall yet be happy."

She gave a cry of satisfaction, and her eyes brightened with a flash of vague intelligence.

"She knows me!—Stephanie!"

His heart swelled; his eyelids were wet with tears. Then, suddenly, the countess showed him a bit of sugar she had found in his pocket while he was speaking to her. He had mistaken for human thought the amount of reason required for a monkey's trick. Philippe dropped to the ground unconscious. Monsieur Fanjat found the countess sitting on the colonel's body. She was biting her sugar, and testifying her pleasure by pretty gestures and affectations with which, had she her reason, she might have imitated her parrot or her cat.

"Ah! my friend," said Philippe, when he came to his senses, "I die every day, every moment! I love too well! I could still bear all, if, in her madness, she had kept her woman's nature. But to see her always a savage, devoid even of modesty, to see her—"

"You want opera madness, do you? something picturesque and pleasing," said the doctor, bitterly. "Your love and your devotion yield before a prejudice. Monsieur, I have deprived myself for your sake of the sad happiness of watching over my niece; I have left to you the pleasure of playing with her; I have kept for myself the heaviest cares. While you have slept, I have watched, I have—Go, monsieur, go! abandon her! leave this sad refuge. I know how to live with that dear darling creature; I comprehend her madness, I watch her gestures, I know her secrets. Some day you will thank me for thus sending you away."

The colonel left the old monastery, never to return but once. The doctor was horrified when he saw the effect he had produced upon his guest, whom he now began to love when he saw him thus. Surely, if either of the two lovers were worthy of pity, it was Philippe; did he not bear alone the burden of their dreadful sorrow?

After the colonel's departure the doctor kept himself informed about him; he learned that the miserable man was living on an estate near Saint-Germain. In truth, the baron, on the faith of a dream, had formed a project which he believed would yet restore the mind of his darling. Unknown to the doctor, he spent the rest of the autumn in preparing for his enterprise. A little river flowed through his park and inundated during the winter the marshes on either side of it, giving it some resemblance to the Beresina. The village of Satout, on the heights above, closed in, like Studzianka, the scene of horror. The colonel collected workmen to deepen the banks, and by the help of his memory, he copied in his park the shore where General Eble destroyed the bridge. He planted piles, and made buttresses and burned them, leaving their charred and blackened ruins, standing in the water from shore to shore. Then he gathered fragments of all kinds, like those of which the raft was built. He ordered dilapidated uniforms and clothing of every grade, and hired hundreds of peasants to wear them; he erected huts and cabins for the purpose of burning them. In short, he forgot nothing that might recall that most awful of all scenes, and he succeeded.

Toward the last of December, when the snow had covered with its thick, white mantle all his imitative preparations, he recognized the Beresina. This false Russia was so terribly truthful, that several of his army comrades recognized the scene of their past misery at once. Monsieur de Sucy took care to keep secret the motive for this tragic imitation, which was talked of in several Parisian circles as a proof of insanity.

Early in January, 1820, the colonel drove in a carriage, the very counterpart of the one in which he had driven the Comte and Comtesse de Vandieres from Moscow to Studzianka. The horses, too, were like those he had gone, at the peril of his life, to fetch from the Russian outposts. He himself wore the soiled fantastic clothing, the same weapons, as on the 29th of November, 1812. He had let his beard grow, also his hair, which was tangled and matted, and his face was neglected, so that nothing might be wanting to represent the awful truth.

"I can guess your purpose," cried Monsieur Fanjat, when he saw the colonel getting out of the carriage. "If you want to succeed, do not let my niece see you in that equipage. To-night I will give her opium. During her sleep, we will dress her as she was at Studzianka, and place her in the carriage. I will follow you in another vehicle."

About two in the morning, the sleeping countess was placed in the carriage and wrapped in heavy coverings. A few peasants with torches lighted up this strange abduction. Suddenly, a piercing cry broke the silence of the night. Philippe and the doctor turned, and saw Genevieve coming half-naked from the ground-floor room in which she slept.

"Adieu, adieu! all is over, adieu!" she cried, weeping hot tears.

"Genevieve, what troubles you?" asked the doctor.

Genevieve shook her head with a motion of despair, raised her arm to heaven, looked at the carriage, uttering a long-drawn moan with every sign of the utmost terror; then she returned to her room silently.

"That is a good omen!" cried the colonel. "She feels she is to lose her companion. Perhaps she SEES that Stephanie will recover her reason."

"God grant it!" said Monsieur Fanjat, who himself was affected by the incident.

Ever since he had made a close study of insanity, the good man had met with many examples of the prophetic faculty and the gift of second sight, proofs of which are frequently given by alienated minds, and which may also be found, so travellers say, among certain tribes of savages.

As the colonel had calculated, Stephanie crossed the fictitious plain of the Beresina at nine o'clock in the morning, when she was awakened by a cannon shot not a hundred yards from the spot where the experiment was to be tried. This was a signal. Hundreds of peasants made a frightful clamor like that on the shore of the river that memorable night, when twenty thousand stragglers were doomed to death or slavery by their own folly.

At the cry, at the shot, the countess sprang from the carriage, and ran, with delirious emotion, over the snow to the banks of the river; she saw the burned bivouacs and the charred remains of the bridge, and the fatal raft, which the men were launching into the icy waters of the Beresina. The major, Philippe, was there, striking back the crowd with his sabre. Madame de Vandieres gave a cry, which went to all hearts, and threw herself before the colonel, whose heart beat wildly. She seemed to gather herself together, and, at first, looked vaguely at the singular scene. For an instant, as rapid as the lightning's flash, her eyes had that lucidity, devoid of mind, which we admire in the eye of birds; then passing her hand across her brow with the keen expression of one who meditates, she contemplated the living memory of a past scene spread before her, and, turning quickly to Philippe, she SAW HIM. An awful silence reigned in the crowd. The colonel gasped, but dared not speak; the doctor wept. Stephanie's sweet face colored faintly; then, from tint to tint, it returned to the brightness of youth, till it glowed with a beautiful crimson. Life and happiness, lighted by intelligence, came nearer and nearer like a conflagration. Convulsive trembling rose from her feet to her heart. Then these phenomena seemed to blend in one as Stephanie's eyes cast forth a celestial ray, the flame of a living soul. She lived, she thought! She shuddered, with fear perhaps, for God himself unloosed that silent tongue, and cast anew His fires into that long-extinguished soul. Human will came with its full electric torrent, and vivified the body from which it had been driven.

"Stephanie!" cried the colonel.

"Oh! it is Philippe," said the poor countess.

She threw herself into the trembling arms that the colonel held out to her, and the clasp of the lovers frightened the spectators. Stephanie·burst into tears. Suddenly her tears stopped, she stiffened as though the lightning had touched her, and said in a feeble voice, —

"Adieu, Philippe; I love thee, adieu!"

"Oh! she is dead," cried the colonel, opening his arms.

The old doctor received the inanimate body of his niece, kissed it as though he were a young man, and carrying it aside, sat down with it still in his arms on a pile of wood. He looked at the countess and placed his feeble trembling hand upon her heart. That heart no longer beat.

"It is true," he said, looking up at the colonel, who stood motionless, and then at Stephanie, on whom death was placing that resplendent beauty, that fugitive halo, which is, perhaps, a pledge of the glorious future — "Yes, she is dead."

"Ah! that smile," cried Philippe, "do you see that smile? Can it be true?"

"She is turning cold," replied Monsieur Fanjat.

Monsieur de Sucy made a few steps to tear himself away from the sight; but he stopped, whistled the air that Stephanie had known, and when she did not come to him, went on with staggering steps like a drunken man, still whistling, but never turning back.

General Philippe de Sucy was thought in the social world to be a very agreeable man, and above all a very gay one. A few days ago, a lady complimented him on his good humor, and the charming equability of his nature.

"Ah! madame," he said, "I pay dear for my liveliness in my lonely evenings."

"Are you ever alone?" she said.

"No," he replied smiling.

If a judicious observer of human nature could have seen at that moment the expression on the Comte de Sucy's face, he would perhaps have shuddered.

"Why don't you marry?" said the lady, who had several daughters at school. "You are rich, titled, and of ancient lineage; you have talents, and a great future before you; all things smile upon you."

"Yes," he said, "but a smile kills me."

The next day the lady heard with great astonishment that Monsieur de Sucy had blown his brains out during the night. The upper ranks of society talked in various ways over this extraordinary event, and each person looked for the cause of it. According to the proclivities of each reasoner, play, love, ambition, hidden disorders, and vices, explained the catastrophe, the last scene of a drama begun in 1812. Two men alone, a marquis and former deputy, and an aged physician, knew that Philippe de Sucy was one of those strong men to whom God has given the unhappy power of issuing daily in triumph from awful combats which they fight with an unseen monster. If, for a moment, God withdraws from such men His all-powerful hand, they succumb.

Lector House believes that a society develops through a two-fold approach of continuous learning and adaptation, which is derived from the study of classic literary works spread across the historic timeline of literature records. Therefore, we aim at reviving, repairing and redeveloping all those inaccessible or damaged but historically as well as culturally important literature across subjects so that the future generations may have an opportunity to study and learn from past works to embark upon a journey of creating a better future.

This book is a result of an effort made by Lector House towards making a contribution to the preservation and repair of original ancient works which might hold historical significance to the approach of continuous learning across subjects.

HAPPY READING & LEARNING!

LECTOR HOUSE LLP
E-MAIL: lectorpublishing@gmail.com

www.ingramcontent.com/pod-product-compliance
Lightning Source LLC
LaVergne TN
LVHW090011200726
843493LV00004B/861